for Oonagh

Copyright © 1989, 1998 and 2001 Lucy Cousins

First published as *The Little Dog Laughed* in 1989
by Macmillan Children's Books
This edition first published in 2001 by Campbell Books
an imprint of Macmillan Children's Books
a division of Macmillan Publishers Limited
25 Eccleston Place, London SW1W 9NF
Basingstoke and Oxford
www.macmillan.com
Associated companies throughout the world

ISBN 0 333 78336 0

3 5 7 9 8 6 4 2

A CIP catalogue record for this book is available
from the British Library

Printed in China

Lucy Cousins

More
Nursery Rhymes

Campbell Books

Contents

Hey, diddle, diddle,

The cat and the fiddle,

The cow jumped over the moon.

The little dog laughed

To see such fun,

And the dish ran away with the spoon.

the cat
& the
fiddle

the
dish
ran away
with
the spoon

Dance to your daddy,
My little babby,
Dance to your daddy,
My little lamb.

You shall have a fishy
In a little dishy,
You shall have a fishy
When the boat comes in.

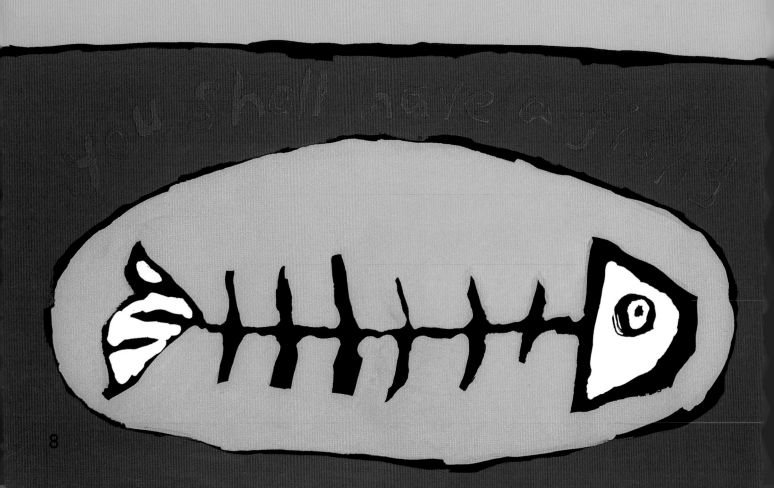

8

Hickory,
    dickory,
        dock,

The mouse ran up the clock.
The clock struck one,
The mouse ran down.

        Hickory,
            dickory,
                dock.

there
was
an old
woman

There was an old woman
Who lived in a shoe,
She had so many children
She didn't know what to do.
She gave them some broth
Without any bread.
She spanked them all soundly
And put them to bed.

Old King Cole

Old King Cole
Was a merry old soul,
And a merry old soul was he.

He called for his pipe,
And he called for his bowl,
And he called for his fiddlers three.

his fiddlers 3

Hickety, pickety, my black hen,
She lays eggs for gentlemen.
Gentlemen come every day
To see what my black hen does lay.

my black hen

Bow-wow, says the dog,
Mew, mew, says the cat,
Grunt, grunt, goes the hog,
And squeak goes the rat.
Tu-whu, says the owl,
Caw, caw, says the crow,
Quack, quack, says the duck,
And what cuckoos say you know.

15

to
see a
fine
lady

upon
a
white
horse

16

Ride a cock horse
To Banbury Cross,
To see a fine lady
Upon a white horse.

With rings on her fingers
And bells on her toes,
She shall have music
Wherever she goes.

This little pig went to market,
This little pig stayed at home,
This little pig had roast beef,
This little pig had none,
And this little pig cried,
"Wee-wee-wee," all the way home.

One, two, three, four, five,

Once I caught a fish alive.

Six, seven, eight, nine, ten,

Then I let it go again.

Why did you let it go?

Because it bit my finger so.

Which finger did it bite?

This little finger on my right.

I saw three ships come sailing by,
Come sailing by, come sailing by,
I saw three ships come sailing by,
On Christmas day in the morning.

And what do you think was in them then,
Was in them then, was in them then?
And what do you think was in them then,
On Christmas day in the morning?

Three pretty girls were in them then,
Were in them then, were in them then,
Three pretty girls were in them then,
On Christmas day in the morning.

One could whistle, and one could sing,
And one could play on the violin;
Such joy there was at my wedding,
On Christmas day in the morning.

I saw three ships

Doctor
Foster
Went to
Gloucester

Doctor Foster went to Gloucester

In a shower of rain.

He stepped in a puddle,

Right up to his middle,

And never went there again.

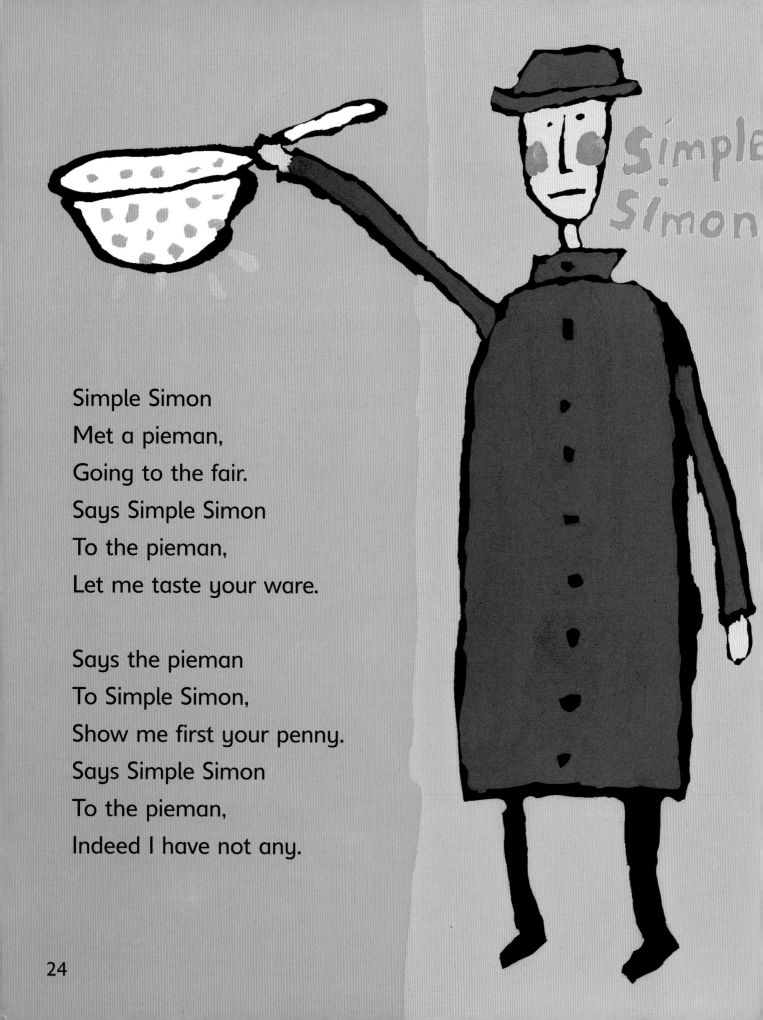

Simple Simon

Simple Simon
Met a pieman,
Going to the fair.
Says Simple Simon
To the pieman,
Let me taste your ware.

Says the pieman
To Simple Simon,
Show me first your penny.
Says Simple Simon
To the pieman,
Indeed I have not any.

Cobbler, cobbler, mend my shoe.
Get it done by half past two.
Stitch it up and stitch it down,
Then I'll give you half a crown.

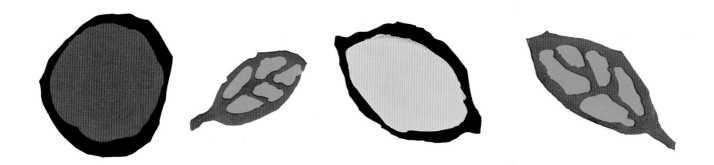

Oranges and lemons,

Say the bells of St Clement's.

You owe me five farthings,

Say the bells of St. Martin's.

When will you pay me?

Say the bells at Old Bailey.

When I grow rich,

Say the bells at Shoreditch.

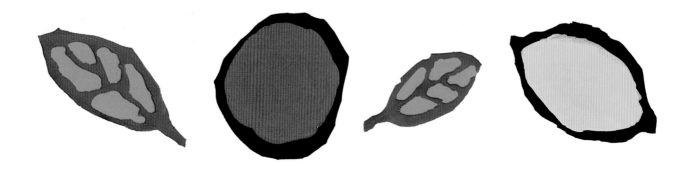

Oranges and lemons

Christmas is coming,
The geese are getting fat.
Please put a penny
In the old man's hat.
If you haven't got a penny,
A ha'penny will do.
If you haven't got a ha'penny,
Then God bless you!

the geese are
getting fat

the north wind doth blow

The north wind doth blow,
And we shall have snow,
And what will poor
  Robin do then,
Poor thing?

He'll sit in a barn,
And keep himself warm,
And hide his head
  Under his wing,
Poor thing.

30

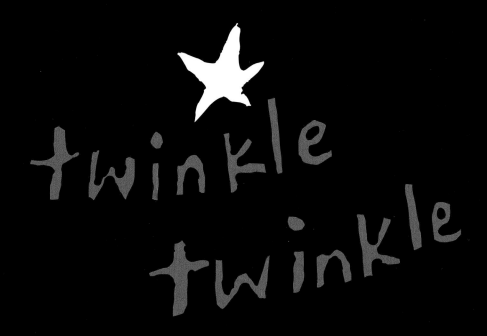

Twinkle, twinkle, little star,
How I wonder what you are!
Up above the world so high,
Like a diamond in the sky.